Tip and Tucker

Paw Painters

Words by **Ann Ingalls** and **Sue Lowell Gallion**

Pictures by André Ceolin

PUBLISHED BY SLEEPING BEAR PRESS

To Lisa, a wonderful teacher and friend
— Sue

For my former students, all 850 of you
— Ann

For Gra, Gabriel, Mela, and for all of our beloved pets
— André

Text Copyright © 2020 Ann Ingalls and Sue Lowell Gallion
Illustration Copyright © 2020 André Ceolin
Design Copyright © 2020 Sleeping Bear Press

Sleeping Bear Press™

2395 South Huron Parkway, Suite 200
Ann Arbor, MI 48104
www.sleepingbearpress.com
© Sleeping Bear Press

Printed and bound in the United States.
10 9 8 7 6 5 4 3 2 1
Library of Congress Cataloging-in-Publication Data
Names: Ingalls, Ann, author. | Gallion, Sue Lowell, author. | Ceolin, Andre, illustrator.
Title: Paw painters / words by Ann Ingalls and Sue Lowell Gallion ; pictures by André Ceolin.
Description: Ann Arbor, MI : Sleeping Bear Press, [2020] | Series: Tip and
Tucker ; [book 3] | Audience: Ages 4-6. | Summary: During art week in
Mr. Lopez's classroom, hamsters Tip and Tucker escape their cage and
make a mess—and some artwork—of their own.
Identifiers: LCCN 2020006365 | ISBN 9781534110991 (hardcover) | ISBN 9781534111004 (paperback)
Subjects: CYAC: Hamsters—Fiction. | Painting—Fiction. | Adventure and
adventurers—Fiction. | Schools—Fiction.
Classification: LCC PZ7.I45 Paw 2020 | DDC [E]—dc23
LC record available at https://lccn.loc.gov/2020006365

Yellow – Amarillo
Blue – Azul
Red – Rojo
Green – Verde
Orange – Anaranjado
Brown – Café
Pink – Rosado
Purple – Morado

"What are we doing today?" asks Emma.

"This is Art Week," Mr. Lopez says.

"We can paint with marbles. Or build with boxes."

"Can we do both?" asks Emma.

"*Sí,*" says Mr. Lopez. "Yes."

Tucker climbs to the top.

To the top of the cage.

"Tip, look at the boxes."

Jayden picks up a marble.
He drops it in the green paint.
"Now drop it on the paper,"
says Mr. Lopez.

Jayden tilts the box up.
He tilts the box down.
"Look what I made!"
"Everyone can be an artist,"
says Mr. Lopez.

Emma gets tubes.

Pim gets boxes.

They build and tape.

"Look! We made a rocket," says Pim.

"For the hamsters," says Emma.

"Nice job," says Mr. Lopez.
"Please put it in the cage."

Tucker climbs up the rocket.

Tip scoots inside.

Just the tip of his tail shows.

"Time for recess," says Mr. Lopez.

"*Vamos, por favor*. Let's go, please."

Tip peeks out.

Out of the rocket.

"Come here, Tip," says Tucker.
Tip climbs
up, up, up.

The rocket tips.
The hamsters tumble.
Out of the cage they go!
BUMP!
THUMP!

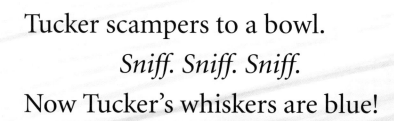

Tucker scampers to a bowl.
Sniff. Sniff. Sniff.
Now Tucker's whiskers are blue!

Tip puts his paw on a cup.

It tips.

It topples.

It spills!

SPLASH!

Now Tip's paws are purple!

Tip scampers away.
He runs fast.
So does Tucker.

Paw prints here.
There.
Everywhere!

The door opens.

"Oh my!" says Mr. Lopez.

"What a mess!" Jayden says.

"Where are Tip and Tucker?"

Emma and Pim run to the cage.

No hamsters here.

"Follow the paw prints," says Pim.

"Hey!" says Carlos.

"Someone nibbled my painting."

"Could it be the hamsters?" asks Emma.

"Over here!" calls Jayden.

"Look at the hole in that bag."

"Oh no!" says Mr. Lopez.

"That is my lunch!"

"Listen," says Pim.

Crunch. Crunch. Crunch.

Everyone laughs.

"What is that noise?" asks Tip.
"I think I know," says Tucker.
He peeks out of the bag.
Tip peeks too.

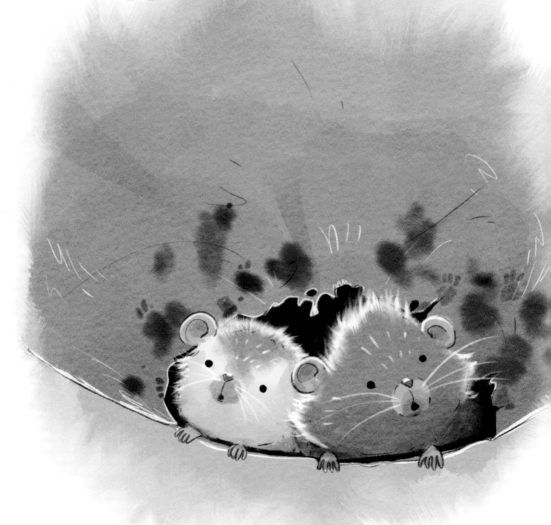

Emma holds out her hands.

Tucker creeps out.

They are nose to nose.

"Your whiskers tickle!" says Emma.

Pim picks up Tip.
"Your paws are purple."

"Now it is cleanup time," says Mr. Lopez.
"For hamsters too," says Carlos.

"Time for a nap," says Tucker.

Honk-shurr, honk-shurr.

Mr. Lopez puts up the art.

BRRIING! The bell rings.

"Lunchtime," says Mr. Lopez.

Out goes the class.

"Wake up, Tucker," says Tip.
"Look on the wall."

Sleepy Tucker looks.
"We are artists too!" Tip says.